RAVEN GOES BERRYPICKING

Anne Cameron

Illustrations by Gaye Hammond

HARBOUR PUBLISHING

5 6 7 8 9 10 — 14 13 12 11 10

Harbour Publishing Co. Ltd.
P.O. Box 219, Madeira Park, BC, V0N 2H0
www.harbourpublishing.com

Cover and book design by Gaye Hammond

Printed and bound in Canada

Harbour Publishing acknowledges financial support from the Government of Canada through the Book Publishing Industry Development Program and the Canada Council for the Arts, and from the Province of British Columbia through the BC Arts Council and the Book Publishing Tax Credit.

Library and Archives Canada Cataloguing in Publication

Cameron, Anne, 1938–
    Raven goes berrypicking

    ISBN 978-1-55017-036-8

    1. Indians of North America—British Columbia—Pacific Coast—Legends—Juvenile literature. 2. Legends—British Columbia—Pacific Coast—Juvenile literature. 3. Ravens—Folklore—Juvenile literature.   I. Hammond, Gaye.   II Title.
E78.N78C34 1990   j398.2'089'970711   C90-091605-2

When I was growing up on Vancouver Island I met a woman who was a storyteller. She shared many stories with me, and later gave me permission to share them with others.

This woman's name was KLOPINUM. In English her name means "Keeper of the River of Copper." It is to her this book is dedicated, and it is in the spirit of sharing, which she taught me, these stories were offered to all small children. I hope you will enjoy them as much as I did.

Anne Cameron

Raven suggested to her friends Gull, Cormorant, and Puffin that they should all go berrypicking.

"We could use your dugout," she said to Cormorant, "and your paddles," she said to Gull, "and gather the berries in your baskets," she said to Puffin.

The friends agreed, and were nice enough not to ask Raven what it was she was going to provide.

Raven sat in Cormorant's dugout and smiled. "I'll hold the baskets," she offered, "so the rest of you can paddle," and the other three, knowing Raven, shrugged and handed her the baskets.

Raven enjoyed the ride, and amused the friends by describing to them all the scenery they were too busy to see and enjoy. "Oh," she said, "look below us, we are over an oyster bed. Why don't we dive for oysters?"

"Wonderful," the others agreed, glad of the chance to stop pulling the paddles and working so hard.

"I don't swim," Raven smiled, "so I'll look after the dugout and you three can dive down and pry the oysters off the rocks and swim up to the surface with them, then I'll take the oysters and open them with my strong beak."

"Well," they thought, "at least she'll be doing Something for a change," and they agreed. One by one they dove over the side of the dugout and swam down to where the oysters clustered on the rocks. They pulled and pried and heaved and strained and managed to break off some, and, one by one, they swam back up to the surface and gave the oysters to Raven, who was lying in the dugout, floating on top of the water, humming a song to herself.

"Thank you," Raven smiled. "I'll open them while you go for more."

Finally, all three were tired and quite chilled by the water, and they swam up and climbed back into the dugout. Raven was lying resting on the baskets, burping and smiling, her belly round and tight as a drum.

"You've eaten them all!" Puffin accused.

"Not so," Raven denied. "See, there are six left; two for each of you." The three friends looked at each other and shrugged.

"Should have known," they told each other.

When they had rested and eaten their two oysters each, they picked up the paddles again, and started off looking for berries.

"Oh, look," said Raven from where she reclined against the baskets. "Look at all the sardines in the kelp beds. We could stop here and you could catch sardines and we could all share. I don't swim well, so I'll stay in the dugout and hang onto the kelp and keep the dugout from drifting away."

"Are you going to eat them all?" they asked, remembering the oysters.

"Of course not!" Raven said indignantly. "We will share equally. You can be sure of that."

So the trusting three went over the side again, and chased the sardines through the undersea forest of kelp.

When they had their beaks full, they swam up and dropped the sardines into the dugout.

"One for you," Raven said with a great big smile. "See, I'm putting this in your pile, Gull," and Gull, surprised but pleased, smiled and went back below the surface of the water to catch more. "And one for me," Raven laughed, popping a sardine in her mouth. "And one for Cormorant, and one for me, and one for Puffin, and one for me," and for every sardine she gave any of the others, she fed herself.

"We ought to have enough," Puffin said, "we've been fishing for over two hours."

They climbed back in the dugout and looked at the three little piles of sardines. "Is that ALL?" they said.

"Equal shares," Raven agreed, her belly swollen bigger than ever. "One for Gull and one for me and one for Puffin and one for me and one for Cormorant and one for me . . ."

"Trickster!" Puffin said, and Raven laughed. "You got three!"

"So did you," Raven reasoned.

"But there are three of us so it's only one each."

"Equal shares," Raven insisted, burping.

The three friends ate their sardines and glared at greedy Raven and vowed to themselves and each other that they weren't going to be tricked again.

They paddled to a small island and beached the dugout on the shore, then took their baskets and began to gather berries. Salmonberries, huckleberries, blackberries, twinberries, salal berries, and oregon grapes, they gathered and stored in their baskets.

Raven picked berries too, but she didn't put hers in the basket. She ate the ones she picked. She munched and she crunched and she chewed and she swallowed and she gorped and she stuffed herself until even she thought she was going to split right down the middle.

"Ooooooooooh," she moaned.

"What's wrong?" asked Puffin.

"Oh, I feel TERRIBLE!" Raven moaned.

"Small wonder," Cormorant said with absolutely no sign of sympathy at all.

"Gluttony is its own worst enemy," Gull pontificated.

"Got what you deserved," little Puffin muttered.

"Oh, I can't pick any more berries," Raven groaned. She hobbled to the dugout and lay down in it, but she couldn't get comfortable. She grizzled and whined and moaned and complained and felt very sorry for herself the whole time the others were picking berries.

"My baskets are full," said Puffin.

"Mine too," said Gull.

"Mine too," said Cormorant.

"Raven's aren't full, we can use them, she isn't going to be picking any more berries today, she's too sick," Puffin suggested.

So the other three picked until even Raven's baskets were full.

And the whole time they were working, Raven was moaning with bellyache.

They loaded the baskets into the dugout and got in. "I can't paddle," Raven gasped, "I'm too sick."

"Figures," Puffin grumbled.

Raven lay in the dugout feeling sorry for herself while the others did all the work. "I'm so thirsty," she whined, "I have got to have a drink of water or I'll die."

So the other three paddled to a place where there was fresh water.

"I can't walk to the pool," Raven protested.

"She's up to something," Puffin warned.

"She's not feeling well," Cormorant defended.

"She's up to something," Puffin insisted.

But the three friends went to get Raven a drink of water. While they were gone, Raven ate all the berries in the baskets she hadn't filled herself.

"I told you," Puffin said when she saw the empty baskets.

"You loaned those baskets to me," Raven argued, "so the berries in them were mine."

"You didn't pick them!" Gull said very very angrily. "We picked them!"

"They were my baskets," Raven insisted stubbornly.

Raven drank the water they had brought and then lay down and put her wing over her eyes. "The sun," she said, "it's hurting my eyes. Oh, I feel so terribly ill."

"Here," said Cormorant, "we'll pile these baskets and you can lie in the shade."

"She's up to something," Puffin warned again.

"What can she do now, sick as she is?" Cormorant asked.

"She's up to something."

And while the other three did all the paddling, Raven poked a hole in a basket and ate the berries. When that basket was empty, she started on another basket.

"Look at that," Puffin whispered to Gull and Cormorant. "See what she's up to now?"

"Glutton," said Cormorant.

"Trickster," said Gull.

"She isn't the only one who can play tricks," Puffin said. And she dug her paddle deep into a wave and turned the dugout sideways so the sun hit Raven right in the eyes.

"Oh, oh, oh," Raven wailed. "Oh, the sun gives me a headache."

"Here," Puffin said, "throw this blanket over your head and shade your eyes." And Raven did.

Immediately Puffin jumped up, pulled a strong cord from where it had been stored, and tied Raven inside the blanket. And to be sure no more of the berries disappeared, she took two turns around Raven's greedy beak. "There," she said with satisfaction, "that'll hold you." And to be sure that it did, she jumped up and down on Raven.

Inside the blanket, Raven began to sweat until she sweated out all the water she had been given. She even sweated out the juice of all the berries she had eaten. She became very very thirsty and very sad. She sweat and sweat until she really did have a bellyache and a headache and her eyes really did hurt. All the things she had pretended to have wrong with her actually did go wrong, and she was very very ill.

When they got back to the village they stood up and dropped their paddles on the blanket-wrapped Raven and gave her lumps, bumps, and bruises. "Oh, oh, oh," Raven cried. "Why are you doing this to me?"

"Because you are a glutton," said Gull.

"Because you are a cheat," said Cormorant.

"Because you are always up to something," said Puffin.

They told all the other creatures all the things Raven had done. "Either we will banish you and nobody will ever talk to you again or play with you or be friends with you, or you will have to make up for what you've done," the creatures decided.

Raven didn't want to live her life all alone. "Anything," she said. "I'm sorry, I truly am."

"Not as sorry as you are going to be," little Puffin promised.

For four days they took Raven back to the berry island, and Raven had to do all the work. She had to paddle the dugout and go over the side for oysters, she had to catch sardines and then fill all the berry baskets while the others lay in the sun and enjoyed life. And to be sure Raven didn't eat anything, they tied her beak up with the strong cord Puffin had provided.

"I'm sorry," Raven repeated, but nobody listened to her.

"I'll be good," she promised, but nobody listened.

"I've learned my lesson," she vowed, but the three friends looked at each other and then at Raven.

"She's up to something," said Puffin.

"She's already figuring out another trick," said Gull.

"She's got that look in her eye," said Cormorant.

Raven flew to the top of a tree and sat in it feeling very lonely and sad. "Nobody trusts me," she cawed to herself. "Nobody trusts me at all."

OTHER BOOKS BY ANNE CAMERON

FOR CHILDREN
How Raven Freed the Moon
How the Loon Lost Her Voice
Orca's Song
Raven Returns the Water
Spider Woman
Lazy Boy
Raven & Snipe
T'aal: The One Who Takes Bad Children
The Gumboot Geese

FOR ADULTS
Earth Witch (poetry)
The Annie Poems (poetry)
Dzelarhons (legends)
Women, Kids & Huckleberry Wine (short stories)
Tales of the Cairds (legends)
South of an Unnamed Creek (novel)
Bright's Crossing (short stories)
Escape to Beulah (novel)
Stubby Amberchuk & the Holy Grail (novel)
Kick the Can (novel)
A Whole Brass Band (novel)
Deejay & Betty (novel)
The Whole Fam Damily (novel)
Selkie (novel)
Aftermath (novel)
Those Lancasters (novel)
Sarah's Children (novel)
Daughters of Copper Woman (novel)
Hardscratch Row (novel)
Family Resemblances (novel)
Dahlia Cassidy (novel)
Dreamspeaker (novel)